Contents

A Note from the Author

When I saw Dolly the Sheep staring out at me from the front page of the newspaper a few years ago I knew right away that I wanted to make up a story from that headline.

FIRST SUCCESSFUL ANIMAL CLONING!

I read the report. It was all about how some clever people had managed to clone a sheep. A sheep! I felt very let down. If I got a chance to clone something, then I would make it something a lot more exciting than a sheep. But what if I tried to clone something and it all went wrong?

I began to write my story. I called it *Mutant...*

This book is for
the Damesick Family –
Jane, Peter, Emily, and Dominic

Mutant

by

Theresa Breslin

Illustrated by Harriet Buckley

First published in 2005 in Great Britain by
Barrington Stoke Ltd
www.barringtonstoke.co.uk

First published in different form by A & C Black Ltd 1998

Reprinted 2006

ISBN-10: 1-84299-336-4
ISBN-13: 978-1-84299-336-1

Printed by in Great Britain by Bell & Bain Ltd

Chapter 1
A Shadow Follows ...

"Blast!"

Brad stopped on the steps outside the Clone Unit where he worked. He'd just looked at his watch to check the time and had seen that it was missing.

"Blast!" he said again. "I must have left it in the locker room."

Now he would have to go back into the unit to get it. The lockers were on the far side of the research labs. He ran up the steps and logged in his personal number to open the door.

His work-mates, Jade and Mark, had gone home. He must hurry. Rob, the security man, would soon lock up the whole place and set the alarms for the night.

Brad made his way past the research tables. He didn't need to switch on the main lights. There was plenty of light coming through the windows from the street-lamps, so he could see where he was going.

He went past the Mutant Human Parts Room. This was where they kept the deformed organs they had used for research in the past. They were locked up in sealed tanks.

Professor Mace, the Head of the Clone Unit, had shown them to Brad when he first came. Brad knew that the mutant organs could never get out of the tanks, but he always felt unhappy when he was near the room where they were kept. Some of the results of past research had been mega-weird. That was before they'd cracked the secrets of genetic cloning!

Brad ran on.

On the wall behind him a shadow followed.

Chapter 2
Fire!

The locker room was at the far end of
the lab.

Brad went inside. He put out his hand
to turn on the light. Then he saw that the
light in the locker room was already on.

"That's funny ..." Brad said softly to himself. "I'm sure I put out all the lights when I left."

Brad knew he'd been the last one to leave. Even Jade, who often worked late, had gone by the time his work was all done.

He smiled, thinking about Jade. She was a real stunner, with her dark hair and deep green eyes. He liked her a lot. Even if the others were a bit put off by the fact that she did not smile when she spoke to them.

Brad went over to his locker and opened it up. His watch wasn't there. Maybe he'd dropped it on the floor? He bent down. There it was! Under the bench.

As Brad stooped to pick up his watch he was aware that there was a strange smell in the room. He sniffed the air and looked around. The smell was coming from one of the air vents at floor level. A long wisp of smoke drifted out of the air vent. Something was burning!

Brad got to his feet at once and went to the exit door. He turned the handle to open it. It didn't move.

The smoke was getting thicker and the smell of burning stronger. Brad put his back to the door and pushed hard. It still didn't move.

The door was stuck.

He was trapped in the lab and it was on fire!

Chapter 3
Trapped!

"Help!" Brad yelled out. "Help! Somebody help me!"

There was no answer. Everyone had gone home. There was nobody there to hear him. Brad looked round in despair ... and spotted the fire alarm on the wall. He

put out his hand, smashed the glass, and pressed the red button.

Nothing happened. Brad gazed at it. Why didn't the alarm go off?

He banged his fist on the wall. The alarm stayed silent. Thick smoke was rising from the floor. It stung Brad's eyes and he began to choke. The smoke filled the room fast. Soon there would be no air left. What could he do?

Brad tore off his jacket, and crammed it against the air vent. But it did not stop the thick smoke from getting through.

Brad panted, gulping for air. He could hardly see. Somehow he got to his feet and fell against the door. He was about to pass out when he heard a voice calling him.

"Brad! Brad! Are you in there?"

The door crashed open and Brad was face to face with ...

Chapter 4
Rescue

"Jade!"

Brad choked out the name and fell forwards.

Jade grabbed his arm. "Are you OK?" she asked him.

"I'll be fine in a moment," said Brad, still panting. "There's a fire in the air vent in the locker room. I couldn't get the door open and the alarm isn't working."

Jade pulled the red fire pump from the wall of the lab, ran into the locker room, and aimed the hose at the air vent.

When she had put out the fire, Jade smiled at Brad. "Most of the smoke's gone now," she said. "It was lucky for you that I came back to the lab to fetch a bag that I'd left behind."

"You're right," said Brad. "I'm glad you heard me. I couldn't get out of the locker room. The door was stuck." He took a good look at the door catch. "It seems all right. Why couldn't I open it just now?"

"I think this is why." Jade took a screw-driver from her pocket. "This was jammed under the door from the outside. I had to yank it free before I could open the door to let you out."

Brad gazed at the screw-driver in Jade's hand. "It didn't roll under the door by itself. Someone must have put it there." He looked at Jade. "Why was it in your pocket?" he asked her.

Jade's face went red. "I ... I don't know," she said. "I must have put it in there after I picked it up."

Brad took the screw-driver from Jade and went into the locker room. "I'm going to get the cover off the air vent," he said. "I want to see what started the fire. There's something very odd about all of this."

Chapter 5
Who is the Spy?

Jade looked on while Brad took the cover off the air vent.

Brad put his hand inside the opening and brought out a bundle of rags. "These smell of petrol," he said.

"Rob, the new security man, should have checked this room," said Jade. "Why didn't he smell the smoke?"

"I don't think he locks up until later," said Brad. He held up the rags. "The person who planned this fire didn't want to burn down the whole lab. Do you think they only wanted to destroy the research work going on just here?"

Jade put her hand to her mouth. "My desk is right next to the locker room." Her voice shook. "Do you think it's my work on the Growth Culture that they want to destroy? If the smoke had got to my test slides they would have been spoiled again."

"What do you mean *again*?" Brad asked her.

"Don't you remember?" said Jade. "Last week I was looking at new cell growth under a microscope. I went for a break and when I came back most of my slides were on the floor. It was as if someone had thrown them to the ground in a rage."

"I remember," said Brad. "At the time we thought it happened by chance. But now ..." His face was grave. "Don't you see? All these things have happened since we discovered the new Growth Culture."

"The Growth Culture," Jade repeated. "It would speed up spare part surgery so much. Once the tests are done on humans we can tell everyone that we can make new body organs. And new arms and legs could grow within a few days."

"It would help so many people," said Brad.

"That's true," said Jade. Her eyes were unhappy as she added, "But in the wrong hands this could do real harm."

"Tomorrow I'm going to speak to Professor Mace," said Brad. "He's the Head of the Unit and must be told. Someone is trying to destroy our work."

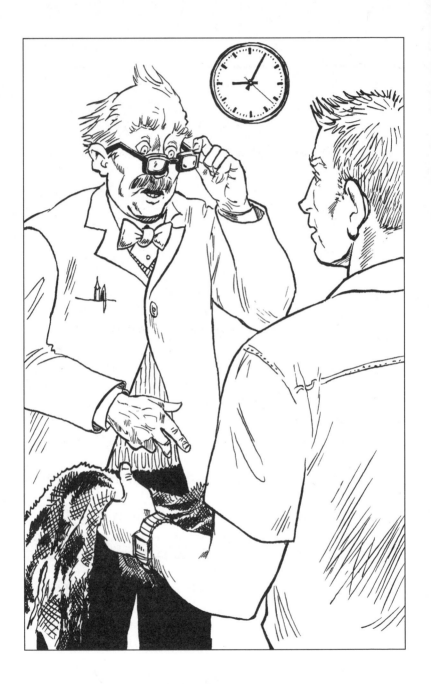

Chapter 6
Sabotage?

The next day Brad showed the petrol soaked rags to Professor Mace, the Head of the Clone Unit.

"Someone is trying to destroy our research!" Professor Mace said.

"Yes," said Brad. "I think someone wants to wreck our experiments on the Growth Culture."

"This is awful," said Professor Mace. His hands shook, and he took off his glasses and wiped them with care.

Then Brad told Professor Mace what had happened in the lab last night.

"This morning I asked Rob, the new security man, to check the fire alarm," Brad went on. "He says someone put it out of action. That's why it didn't go off last night."

"I can't believe it," said Professor Mace. "Our work here is so important. I've spent my whole life in this lab."

Brad saw that the Professor was worn out. He knew that Professor Mace had been with the Clone Unit since it had first opened. It would break his heart if the research went wrong.

"It seems we have a spy among us. Did anyone follow you last night?" the Professor asked Brad.

Brad shook his head.

The Professor gave a sigh. "We'll have to take great care. It's more important than ever now that Jade is about to do tests on humans."

"On humans? I didn't know that we were at that stage," said Brad. "Isn't it a bit risky?"

"We've tried the Growth Culture on some of the animal parts in the Mutant Organs Room and had good results." Professor Mace smiled. "They grew in a matter of hours."

"But who would offer to test the Growth Culture?" asked Brad.

"Me," said a voice from the door.

Chapter 7
The New Growth Culture

Brad turned round.

Mark stood in the open door. He ran his fingers through his hair.

"I told Jade that she can test the Culture on me," Mark said. "So she's setting it up for the end of the week."

33

"I think we might have to put off the tests on humans for the moment. I must speak to Jade about this." The Professor strode out of the room.

"I thought he'd be pleased," said Mark.

"The Professor is very upset about the fire yesterday," Brad told him. "It's such a puzzle. Why would anyone want to mess up our research?"

"It's clear," said Mark. "One day the Growth Culture will be worth millions."

Brad looked at Mark hard as he walked away. Mark seemed very nervous. Was it because he was to be the human test animal in the experiments? Or was he the one who was trying to wreck the research?

Could it be Jade? Last night she'd looked so guilty when she'd taken the screw-driver from her pocket. Had she just forgotten it was there? Or had she jammed it under the door and then taken pity on Brad when she'd heard him shouting for help? Perhaps she'd been scared that Rob, the security man, would hear Brad's yells.

And what about Rob? Didn't he check the fire alarms? Why hadn't he seen that the alarm was out of order? Was it because he was new? Or had he put the alarm out of action himself and started the fire?

Who *was* the person trying to destroy the Growth Culture?

Chapter 8
Missing Computer Files

"The Professor wants me to put off the test on Mark," Jade told Brad the next day. "I don't understand why."

"He's worried about security," said Brad. "And I suppose he wants to make sure that the test will be safe."

"I wouldn't try testing on humans if I didn't think it was safe," said Jade. "Let me show you my test results on the computer."

She turned on her computer and clicked the mouse.

"Oh no!" Jade's face was pale now. "My data!"

In a panic Jade went right through her files. "My data! It's gone! Someone has wiped my files!"

Brad and Jade rushed off to tell Professor Mace of this new disaster.

"That settles it," said the Professor. "We will have to put off the testing of the Growth Culture on humans."

"No," said Jade. "I keep back-up files. We can still do the tests on Mark as planned."

"We should wait," said Professor Mace, "until we find out who is trying to destroy our work."

"I don't agree," said Brad. "I think we must go ahead right away. If we have a spy in the lab then the sooner we do the tests the better."

"Yes," said Jade. "Mark is ready to do it. Let's get it over with before he changes his mind."

"If you're quite sure." Professor Mace wasn't happy but he nodded his head. "Quite, quite sure," he said again. "Then on Friday we will do the human tests."

Chapter 9
First Human Test

On Friday, Brad met Mark and Jade in the locker room.

They put on their clean white overalls and the helmets that they wore in the test room.

Mark's face was shiny with sweat. He was shaking.

Brad remembered that Mark had said that the Growth Culture was worth millions. Had Mark tried to steal Jade's research so that he would be rich?

Professor Mace came into the locker room to wish them luck.

"I'm sorry I can't be there," he said. "I'm off to meet Rob now to talk about security. It can't wait."

He saw that Mark was nervous. "You can change your mind," the Professor told Mark. "This could harm or even kill you."

Kill you.

Brad remembered that Jade had said that about the Growth Culture. How could it harm or kill you?

It would only be used to help people who had lost an arm or a leg or needed a new liver or kidney ... wouldn't it?

Mark took a deep breath.

"I'm fine," he said. "Let's do it."

Chapter 10
Attacked!

In the test room Jade shaved some fine hair and layers of skin from the back of Mark's hand.

She took the stopper out of the small bottle that held the Growth Culture.

"This is the only sample of the Growth Culture that we have," she said.

The mask made Jade's voice sound far away. Her eyes shone like green stars. It can't be her, Brad thought. She wouldn't try to destroy her own research. Would she? Yet ... she had a very bright mind and they did say that genius was close to madness.

Jade placed a tiny, tiny droplet of the Culture on Mark's skin. She put the bottle back on the table.

And waited ...

"I don't believe it!" Brad gaped at Mark's hand.

As soon as the Culture touched Mark's hand cells formed. Skin and hairs grew back at once. At that moment Brad saw why the Culture could be such a danger.

"The Professor must see this," said Brad. "I'll find him."

He turned to the door.

At that moment the lights went out. Brad heard the door open. Someone pushed past him. Then Jade gave a scream.

At once the stand-by lights came on.

Jade was lying on the floor. Mark stood to one side, holding his head.

"What happened?" asked Brad.

"Someone hit me," said Mark.

"Me too," said Jade. She got to her feet. She looked at the table for the bottle that held the Culture. It wasn't there.

"The Culture!" Jade yelled. "The Growth Culture! It's gone! Someone has stolen it!"

Chapter 11

The Growth Culture is Stolen

Brad opened the door.

Rob the security man was standing outside.

"What are you doing here?" Brad wanted to know.

"I heard a scream and came to help. What's wrong?"

"The bottle with the Growth Culture has been stolen," said Brad.

Mark and Jade pushed through the door behind Brad.

Jade grabbed Rob. "Give it back!" she yelled. "You've no idea how much harm it can do. Even a very small amount can make human parts grow much bigger and stronger."

Rob shook her off. "I didn't take the Culture," he said. "I just got here."

"You should be in a meeting with Professor Mace about security," said Mark. "Why aren't you with him?"

"That meeting was yesterday," said Rob.

"Yesterday?" Brad asked. "But the Professor told us he couldn't watch the test because he had to meet up with you."

Rob shook his head. "We spoke about security *yesterday*," he told them.

"Why isn't Professor Mace here?" asked Mark. "He must have heard Jade shout."

"Where is Professor Mace?" asked Jade.

"I saw him as I was running here," said Rob. "He had a small bottle in his hand." And then he added in a scared voice, "He was going into the Mutant Human Parts Room."

Chapter 12
Mutant Madness

"Professor! What are you doing?"

Brad was first to reach the Mutant Human Parts Room. Professor Mace was leaning over one of the tanks. It was open. At the bottom lay a blob of human flesh. It was throbbing.

"Stay back!"

Professor Mace held the bottle with the Growth Culture in his hand.

"Professor, stop!" Jade yelled. "You cannot give the Culture to these mistakes!"

"Mistakes!" Professor Mace gave an evil grin. "These are *mine.* My early work. They should not be kept trapped in here. I can use this ..." He held the bottle with the Culture high above his head. "I can use this to make them strong. They will grow.

Then no-one will be able to keep them shut away."

"He's gone crazy," Rob said in a low voice. "Keep him talking and I'll try to edge round behind him."

Professor Mace took the lid off the bottle. He leaned over the tank. He tilted the bottle ...

Chapter 13
The Lid Opens ...

"No!" Jade shouted.

Mark dived across the room.

Rob rushed to put a hand on the Professor's arm.

Brad grabbed the bottle and clamped the lid down firmly.

"I'll call the hospital," said Rob as he led the Professor away. "I think he needs medical help."

"Let's seal the tank up." Mark closed the lid tight.

The rest of the team left the lab.

"Thank goodness that's over," said Brad.

"I'm glad you got the lid back on the bottle," said Jade. "It would have been a total disaster if any of the Culture had dropped onto that pulsing flesh."

"Well, it didn't happen," said Brad. "So let's not think about it."

Behind the doors of the Mutant Human Parts Room a tiny drop of the Growth Culture trickled down the inside of the sealed glass tank.

A long thin arm slithered along the floor of the tank. It reached out ... looking for something. A pulse throbbed, became stronger. Cells divided and grew, faster and faster.

Hours later, the arm, thicker now and stronger, reached out and up.

It pushed against the top of the tank, and slowly, slowly the lid began to open ...

Barrington Stoke would like to thank all its readers for commenting on the manuscript before publication and in particular:

Jessica Anderson

Claire Brash

Carol Hodgson

Tom O'Shea

Mr Nick Rees

Mathew Rooke

Charlie Shelley

Become a Consultant!

Would you like to give us feedback on our titles before they are published? Contact us at the address below – we'd love to hear from you!

Email: info@barringtonstoke.co.uk
Website: www.barringtonstoke.co.uk